ON THE
EDGE OF THE SEA

Betty Paraskevas

PAINTINGS BY

Michael Paraskevas

Aladdin Paperbacks

First Aladdin Paperbacks edition May 1999

Aladdin Paperbacks
An imprint of Simon & Schuster
Children's Publishing Division
1230 Avenue of the Americas
New York, NY 10020

Typography by Amelia Lau Carling
The art for each picture consists of an acrylic painting,
which is scanner-separated and reproduced in full color.

Printed in Hong Kong
10 9 8 7 6 5 4 3 2 1

The Library of Congress has cataloged the hardcover edition as follows:
Paraskevas, Betty
On the edge of the sea / by Betty Paraskevas ;
paintings by Michael Paraskevas.—1st ed.
p.   cm.
Summary: A boy dreams that he lives in a sand castle on the edge of the sea.
ISBN 0-8037-1130-1 (tr.). — ISBN 0-8037-1263-4 (lib.)
[1. Dreams—Fiction. 2. Seashore—Fiction. 3. Sand castles—Fiction.]
I. Paraskevas, Michael, 1961– ill. II. Title.
PZ7.P2135On 1992 [E]—dc20 91-31489 CIP AC
ISBN 0-689-82533-1 (Aladdin pbk.)

To Paul and Judy, Dr. John Sprowls,
Lucille Sprowls, Stan Goldberg, Hilary Knight,
Justin Cohane, and Rachel Pine

I dreamed I lived on the edge of the sea
In a castle of sand with a window for me,

To watch the sun climb the morning sky,

And count the ships that go sailing by.

I saw my friends making their way

Across the sand, and we spent the day

Riding the waves that rolled up the shore

But always stopped short of my castle door.

With their candy-striped chairs and umbrellas for shade,

I served them all hot dogs and pink lemonade.

Shimmering kites of brilliant designs

Climbing the sky, tugging their lines.

A lady snoozed on a peppermint raft,

Until a wave knocked her off and everyone laughed.

Hundreds of beach balls bounced in the sky.
Everyone cheered and I wondered why

They floated down so graceful and free,
Then burst like bubbles when they touched the sea.

The lifeguard, standing on his lookout chair,
Shouted, "Iceberg offshore! Bathers, *beware!*"

We gathered together and watched it drift by.
There were diamonds on the water and a crystal blue sky.

A mighty gust of wind made a strange whistling sound,
Tossing towels and umbrellas and hats all around.

We picked up our things and when we were done,
We sat on the beach, enjoying the sun.

In pleated paper cups I served them rainbow ices,
Saltwater taffy, and watermelon slices.

Friendships grew through the rest of the day,
While the bright orange sun slowly slipped away.

My friends said "Good night" by the light of the moon.
As they followed the path that crossed the dune,

I hurried to my castle door,
Playing tag with the waves that rushed the shore.

I climbed the tower and stepped into the night.
There were stars 'round my head, the moon was on my right.
The air made me dizzy, stardust made me sneeze,
I lost my favorite hat in a wild, sudden breeze.

I saw it on the moon as I leaned upon the ledge,
But the ledge began to crumble and I tumbled off the edge.
I was falling through the night until my mother said,
"It's time to start a brand-new day! Get up, sleepyhead!"

I never had another dream as wonderful as that,
But sometimes when I see the moon I wonder
Why I never found my hat.